For Mea and Edison
- S. C.

For S. P. the man who loves to build beautiful things
- C. P.

tiger tales
5 River Road, Suite 128, Wilton, CT 06897
Published in the United States 2016
Originally published in Great Britain as *Badger and the Great Rescue*
by Little Tiger Press
Text copyright © 2016 Little Tiger Press
Illustrations copyright © 2016 Caroline Pedler
ISBN-13: 978-1-68010-007-5
ISBN-10: 1-68010-007-6
Printed in China
LTP/1400/1240/0815

10 9 8 7 6 5 4 3 2 1

For more insight and activities,
visit us at www.tigertalesbooks.com

Friends TO THE RESCUE

by Suzanne Chiew • *Illustrated by* Caroline Pedler

tiger tales

One bright day, Badger was busy reading when Mouse raced over to him.

"Badger, look at this rope I found!" she cried. "It's perfect for a clothesline. Will you help me make one?"

"Of course!" smiled Badger.

He picked up his tools and off they went.

In no time at all, Mouse's laundry hung on her brand-new line.

"I wonder where the rope came from," said Badger.
   Then something in the bushes caught his eye. He reached into the leaves and pulled it out.

"It's a basket!" squeaked Mouse.
"It's a mystery!" frowned Badger.
"How did it get here?"

Mouse hopped around excitedly.
"It would make a great house for
Hedgehog!"
Badger nodded. "Let's
surprise him."

They patched and mended
until the house was perfect.
"Hedgehog will be so happy!"
Mouse giggled. And she was right!

"Thank you!" squealed Hedgehog. "It's wonderful!"
"We found it in the bushes," said Mouse.
"That's strange," said Hedgehog. "I've found
something, too. Come with me."

But when they reached the clearing,
Rabbit was already there.
    "Look at my beautiful cloth!" he cried.
"I'm going to make a tent."
    "But I need it to make a hammock!"
said Hedgehog.
    "Can I have some for a kite?"
Mouse asked.

"We can share it," smiled Badger.
"There's plenty to go around."

Rabbit carefully divided
up the cloth.

"Hold on!" frowned Hedgehog.
"Why do you have the biggest
piece?"

"Because I'm the biggest," said Rabbit.
"But I found it first!" huffed Hedgehog.
"And my piece is too small to make anything!" Mouse sniffed.
The friends started to bicker, and soon there was a terrible argument.

"STOP!" said Badger. "There's no
need to argue. We can share
the cloth equally. Look."
He divided the cloth into three
equal pieces.
"Hooray!" everyone cheered.

"I'll start cutting," beamed Rabbit.
But just then Bird swooped down.
"Quick, quick!" she chirped.
"Someone needs our help!"

They followed Bird to the tallest tree in the forest. There, clinging to a branch, was a frightened little mole.

"Help!" he yelled. "HELP!"
"How terrible!" fretted Rabbit.
"What can we do?" squeaked Mouse.
Badger frowned. "We must rescue him!"

"I could try to carry him down," offered Bird. "But I might not be strong enough."

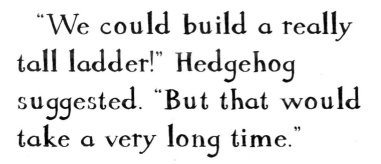

"We could build a really tall ladder!" Hedgehog suggested. "But that would take a very long time."

"I know!" said Rabbit. "Mole can jump and we'll catch him in that piece of cloth!"
They all rushed off to get it.

The friends stretched out the cloth
like a huge trampoline.
"Jump, Mole!" shouted Badger.
"We'll catch you!"

But when Mole looked down he couldn't believe his eyes. "My hot air balloon!" he cried.

"A balloon?" gasped Badger. "That's where all those useful things came from!"

"I tumbled out when my balloon bumped into this tree," called Mole. "I thought I'd lost it forever."

"Don't worry!" shouted Badger. "We'll fix your balloon—and use it to rescue you!"

"I'm sorry there'll be no new clothesline or house," said Badger as they collected the pieces of Mole's hot air balloon. "We don't mind," the friends replied. "We must help Mole!"

Everyone went to work.
They knotted and tied,

and stitched and glued,

until the balloon was
as good as new.

"We're coming, Mole!" called Rabbit as the balloon sailed up, up, upward.

At the top of the tree, Badger reached out with a strong, friendly paw. "Don't be frightened, Mole," he said. "Just hold on tight."

"You won't let go?" whispered Mole.
"I promise," said Badger.
And with a WHOOSH, he pulled
Mole to safety.

"What great new friends you are!"
beamed Mole. "How can I ever thank you?"

"Well—" said Badger.

"We were hoping you'd take us for a ride!"
laughed Rabbit.

"That's a wonderful idea!" giggled Mole.
"Away we go!"

And they all floated off toward
a brand-new adventure.